For André and Noelle

Library of Congress catalog card number: 2020941857
ISBN: 978-1-7353521-0-7 (Paperback)
978-1-7353521-4-5 (Hardback)
978-1-7353521-1-4 (Ebook)

MIKAELA WILSON
—— BOOKS INC. ——

ANDRÉ
The Best
Big Brother

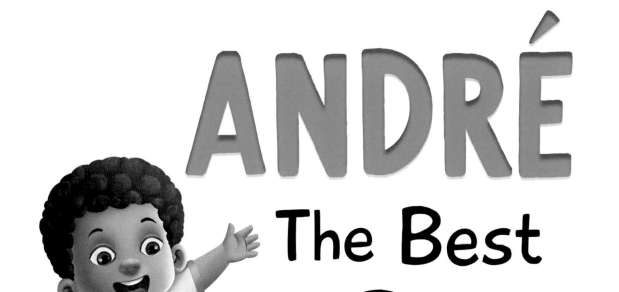

Written by
Mikaela Wilson

Illustrated by
Pardeep Mehra

Art Direction and Storyboards by
Mikaela Wilson

The sun is just beginning to shine
as André jumps out of bed.

"Today I'm going to be a big brother!"

"Mom and Dad said we'll have a new baby today.
I'm going to be the best big brother."

André brushes his teeth...

"WHOOPS!"

...and puts on his best
"big brother"
clothes.

He makes a pile of his favorite books
to read to the new baby.

He picks out his favorite toys to share with the new baby.

He even sets aside his favorite teddy bear to show the new baby.

André hears his dad calling,

"Mom is home!"

He goes downstairs, carrying his favorite teddy bear.

"André, come and meet the new baby,"
Mom says.

André feels sad when he sees his mom holding the new baby in her arms.

He wonders if he really wants this new baby.

"That's MY mom!!!"

André screams, as tears run down his face.

"Of course I'm YOUR mom, honey," his mom says,

"and I'm the new baby's mom, too."

André's dad picks him up
and gives him a big hug.

That makes André
feel much better.

"Would you like to hold the new baby?"
André's mom asks.

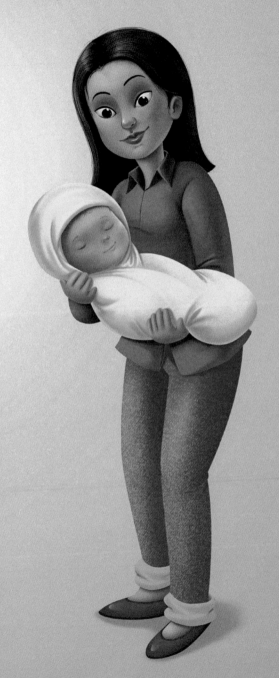

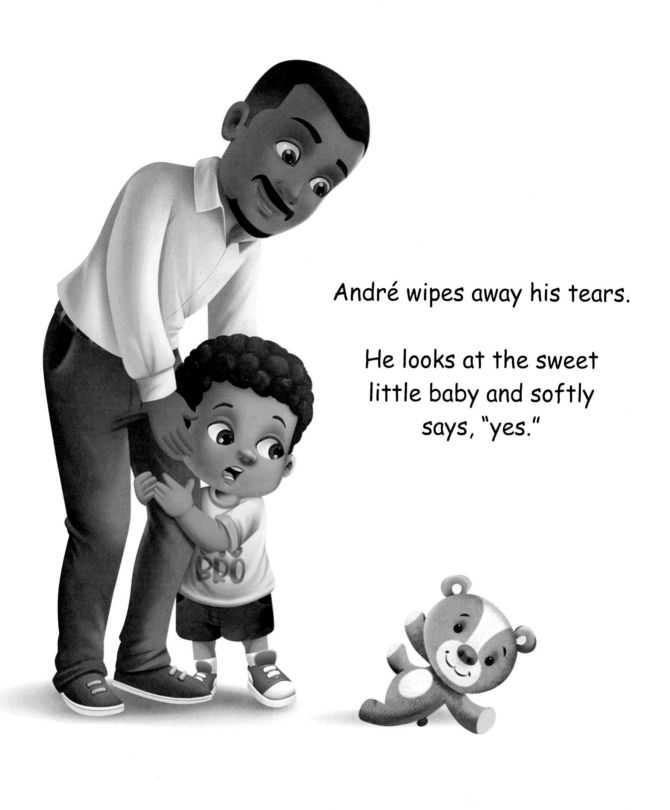

André wipes away his tears.

He looks at the sweet
little baby and softly
says, "yes."

André's dad helps him sit on the couch and hold his arms out.

His mom gently places the baby in his arms.

André's mom smiles as she helps him cradle the baby in his arms. The baby is so small and cuddly.

André loves the baby.

After dinner, André is ready for his usual playtime with Mom and Dad.

"Mom! Dad! Let's play!"

But his parents are busy taking care of the new baby.

André sits in his room, wondering what to do.

"Wait, I can help with the new baby!"

André runs into the baby's room.

"Mom, can I help feed the new baby?" he asks.
"Sure!" says Mom. She lets André help hold the baby's bottle.

"Dad, can I help change the baby's diaper?"
he asks. "Sure," says Dad.

André gets a clean diaper
and gives it to his dad.

(peeee-eww!)

André even throws the
dirty one in the trash.

André shows the baby the books he has set aside and the toys he has picked out.

He has the best night with his mom and dad and the new baby.

André even sings a sweet, bedtime song to the new baby.

Then he kisses the baby on the cheek and whispers,

"I love you, baby."

The baby coos at him and drifts off to sleep.

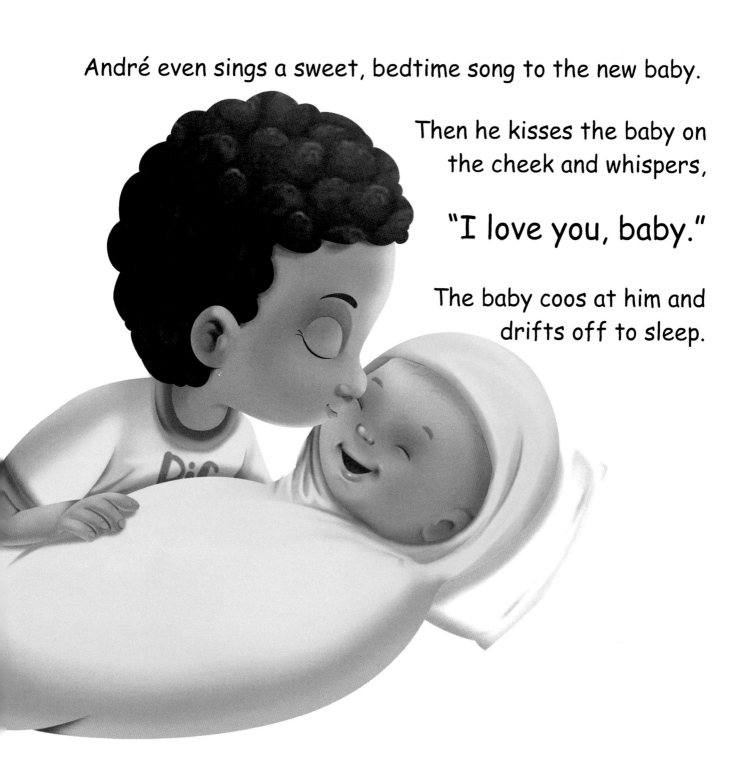

The next morning, the sun is just beginning to shine when André jumps out of bed.

He runs right to the new baby's room.
André loves being the best big brother.

André

Noelle

Dear Reader,

I hope you enjoyed reading this book!
If you have a moment to spare, please drop a quick
review on Amazon. I'm grateful for all the feedback!
If you have any questions or comments please email
mikaelawilsonbooks@gmail.com

Be the first to know about new book releases
and grab your free coloring pages at

www.mikaelawilsonbooks.com

 @mikaelawilsonbooks

 Mikaela Wilson Books

About the Author

Mikaela Wilson

Mikaela Wilson is an author on a mission to bring fun, entertaining and meaningful stories to children's lives. In addition to working full-time as an IT Application Analyst, she is a wife and a mother of two young children. After reading countless children's books with her kids, she saw a need for more diversity in children's books and was inspired to create her own. The Live, Laugh Grow series is modeled after her own multicultural family. Mikaela hopes her books will be timeless and families can read and enjoy them for years to come.

About the Illustrator

Pardeep Mehra

Pardeep Mehra is the founder of Pencil Master Digital Studio, a family-owned business employing a large group of talented artists providing end-to-end illustration and publishing services. For more than 15 years, Pardeep has been providing his keen eye, visualization and digital art skills to create books that delight children all over the world. Pardeep lives in India with his wife and daughter. For more info visit www.pencilmasterdigi.com

Made in the USA
Las Vegas, NV
31 August 2021